DIARY OF A
SPACEPERSON

DIARY OF A
SPACEPERSON
CHRIS FOSS

Paper Tiger

A Dragon's World Ltd Imprint

Dragon's World Ltd
Limpsfield
Surrey RH8 0DY
Great Britain

British Library Cataloguing in Publication Data

Foss, Chris
Diary of a spaceperson.
I. Title
823.914 [F]

ISBN 1 85028 048 7 (hardback)
ISBN 1 85028 049 5 (limpback)

Typeset by Dragon's World Ltd
Printed in Spain
Grafman, S. A.

Publisher's Note

The contents of this book represent an amalgam of extracts from a large diary found whilst the New Venice site was being excavated. The dates bear no relation to known calendars and carbon dating has so far been unsuccessful in identifying the age of the physical material.

J (who never mentions her whole name) is obviously a typically bubbly student. For various reasons she gets herself into all sorts of fixes that nowadays would be less serious, but in the worlds she moved through, clearly could lead to serious consequences.

Where possible drawings are incorporated in relation to the relevant text, but at times J rambles and chronological order is not maintained. This is hardly surprising when one considers that she appears to have attempted regular entries despite her various adventures.

Self-portrait

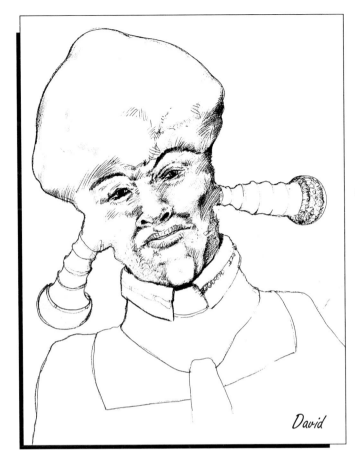

David

ALPHADEN 08   12.10.90

This morning David, my tutor, looked at me thru those lo-lite lenses of his and said, I thought a little sadly, 'You know J, one of the great tragedies of your life is that you missed the draft'. For the first time he had said something that made me think! Maybe that's the reason why I've finally started this diary. Trouble is, I'll have to carry on now — HO HUM!

ALPHADEN 10   02.12.90

Officially it's the first day of spring. Looking outside you wouldn't know it. The rain is teeming down. It's the first of the year so the roofs opposite are streaked and slimy as it mixes with the dust. Roz, my room mate is still asleep. She snores badly. I'm used to it so normally it doesn't bother me. But tonight of all nights it's driving me mad — how she can sleep so soundly when tomorrow is our finals is beyond me. Needless to say, neither of us have done a jot but if things go as usual Roz will sail through and I will flunk. She will go on to Echo 10 and I will be stuck here with the new intake. It's not fair.

ALPHADEN 14   06.21.90

I'm not exactly nervous, mildly terrified would be more accurate. I'm due to see David at 10.00. It's too early for the results but he knows something. He always addresses me as Cadet when it's heavy and let's face it, the only time he DOES see me is when it's heavy. I really haven't done anything recently. It was Roz who did the last takeaway, I just went for the ride. And she admitted it was her!! I haven't used anyone else's card for ages and I'm not far over-limit on my allowance — SO WHAT IS IT?

ALPHADEN 15   19.88.95

I don't believe it. I REALLY DON'T BELIEVE IT!! They can't do this to me. That bald-headed old sod has assigned me to Venice. That land of DIVS, PEABRAINS and NO HOPERS. What's more I can't stand water, leastways what passes for water up here. Thank God we don't have to drink the stuff.

I said I was prepared to be held back but he said I had wrecked every class I deigned to attend on those rare occasions there was no alternative entertainment. And he said I'd damaged more equipment than the whole of the rest of the intake put together. On top of that he said my genes were so far out of synch they couldn't even consider me for maternity service. BABIES, YUGH!!

109.88.90

Still boiling. Spent the last hour trying to hack a virus into the system. I was trying to break into the command channel for the tanker moorings to get one of those blimps to break loose and carry away the markers for tomorrow's assignment WHICH I SHALL NOT BE ATTENDING.

Roz is out looking for supplies, but what with everyone (except someone I know) out celebrating their passes it's suddenly hard to come by — all our reliable sources have dried up.

119.88.90

Certainly the last entry for today, maybe a century! Roz struck gold, best quality we've ever hit: I am really flying. The rest of them are pasted on the walls and I can see right into their heads — ho hum. Goodbye book.

Finnegan's Folly

Miki

ALPHADEN 17 01.19.91

Found this sketch from the UP country walk. During the great war the army built mock terrain for training. This was known as Finnegan's Folly after some old character who took it over after the war. He tried to raise kelper, but our gravity was too much and the project died.

    This is Miki — I don't know her very well. She's on nursing but we get on well at parties and most of her friends can get strike — useful connection. She's already signed up to be a doctor on Faro. Sooner her than me.

ALPHADEN 21 32.18.91

Taking flight training more seriously. Departure looms and the prospect of being solo in deep space is fast becoming a reality. My theory is hopeless and I don't bother going to navigation. After all, most ships have at least three backups so the chances of me having to numerize are remote.

ALPHADEN 26 14.70.91

Lousy day. Fed up with everyone. I actually attended ETU and in my opinion did a neat core analysis when Shark sprang a total shutdown on us. Bearing in mind there's never been a shutdown anywhere in living memory, I thought it was absolutely unreal.

Sal in normal state

Another bad day — they know I'm really trying but I suppose all the years of bunking off have left me with a reputation it's too late to shift. I got to course analysis on time in kit. But admittedly without prep — how could I? I wasn't there for that (most boring part of studies). Also, I have to admit due to the early hour I'd had a little snort. Dialysis picked up on that so I was relegated to a PM shot. Shorty very reluctantly let me go but I persuaded him and frankly didn't think I did too badly — at least until the time sheets came down: I was more than two hours behind the junior mean. I can't win.

Sal the praying mantis!

Something completely different to cheer me up. This is Sal — the course smoothie. She's hitting an outleader blatantly. Everyone knows. I don't know how she gets away with it except he bunged her a strobe: it does the change in 5 minutes. It's absolutely incredible. The problem with Sal is that she's so damn unreliable! For instance, we play scat each quarter day on level 10 — no problem, but she does change even for that. I know I'm not punctual, but she's unreal, anything up to two hours! She's very patronizing — usually wins then wafts off to mix with the big people — fully changed so no chance of being spotted. Still, Alice says she won't make 50 before total breakdown — something to do with bones being unable to reknit. And the old grey stuff doesn't like the constant tampering either.

Sal in change

I'm just not the academic type. I quite like practicals when I can do it my way in my time — but course theory, yawn!! Today we are doing bending movement calcs on old SU beams. They've been obsolete for more than a century, so it's hard to see the relevance. Seeing Sal tonight and she's going to take me uplevel. It's worth the risk and with so little time left, I'm very curious.

9

58.20

Amazing trip! Sal didn't have the kit for a full change but did a simple zero. I really liked myself. Most of the folk were outsiders — very sophisticated. Think I acquitted myself quite well and didn't get too smashed. Met some flight crew just back from Polar Bear and weedled a little ball of strike. Should last at least an orbit on present consumption. Sal very blatant towards the end — so she's not THAT sophisticated.

61.30

Awoken by a call from Sal — she was completely nude between two outers and well gone. Said if I came back up I could earn a grand. Said I'd lost the pass and anyway was almost asleep, glad I left when I did! Beginning to understand why Sal's always got money — will avoid her before depart.

Sarah

ALPHADEN 40   21.08.91

I've been on Venice three days now. Things could be worse.
The room is larger than I expected and I share it with
Sarah — quite the opposite to Roz who I miss desperately.
I'll be turning to the book quite a lot I should think. I'm
definitely not cut out for the marine life — if only I hadn't
pissed about so much! The main difference here is that I am
no longer the eternal student. I'm very definitely working!
WATER, at least Venice's version of water — I DO NOT LIKE
IT. It bumps you up and down and is generally unpredictable
and inhospitable. Give me space anytime. To think that I
hankered after the Earth. Mind you, real water would be
different — it would be wet in a pleasant way and not stick

to you and be slow to drain. And Earth's oceans would be full
of real salt water with wind and amazing things like that.
They create winds here, but only by temperature transfer.

ALPHADEN 43   06.21.91

Decided I don't like Sarah. She's incredibly prudish and
keeps herself covered at all times — even in bed. She's got
a lovely figure and when I suggested doing a nude sketch of
her she looked like when I was asking her about supplies.
Begin to wonder whether she reports me to control — could
this be? The monotony is dreadful and since I made it clear
that I do NOT like water I've been given nothing but shitty
assignments. NO FUN, NO STRIKE, NO FRIENDS. Some life!

ALPHADEN 46 21.92.91

This time I really know I've done something. Driven by the constant drivel around me I mixed up my own hooch — think I used too much methol but I was anxious to push the fermentation. Anyway, I've had it brewing in the cabin for three weeks and last night or possibly the one before I gave it a crack. Sarah was not amused so I went on deck. Very pleasant, a good tone and well mulled. I think it was around glass 10 things got out of hand. Dim memory of a fight with some markers. Then down town. Not a good idea. Some teeny mugged me for my chain and contact bracelet. Very dim memories of her having some of my clothes — or something!! Anyway, was definitely topless in the plaza. Then I was in this amazing booth. Some sort of trade fair. This guy had this fantastic book. Ever since I've been here I've been

bitching about water but in this book he had the real thing. It was really AMAZING. He said would I like to see the real sea — the real ocean they have on Earth. He opened these pages and there it was, the OCEAN — it moved and swished and there was foam and spray!!! AND THE SMELL, THE INCREDIBLE SMELL!! Frankly it was a total revelation. Then he said if I signed up with his outfit for five years I'd make it to EARTH! I'd actually beat the stage plan. I think I sighed. God knows what I did, anyway I doubt if it's valid.

70. 86 .109

Went down town to try and find the booth but no sign of it or any familiar location. Perhaps it was a dream. At least I'll be flying tomorrow even if it's only marshalling in the Berg Park. Frozen water — YUGH!

BETADEN 06   07.24.90

A new orbit, perhaps life will be kinder to me. I am getting into the routine a bit. One piece of excitement: I've been in the Berg Park for some time now and they have a great scam selling bergs. The juice gets split through the team and now I've found a source my little strike supply is guaranteed — makes life worth living.

BETADEN 07   10.31.90

Hauled in before a control captain this morning. Thought it was the scam but imagine my shock when these two really weird characters came in.

It seems I really did sign a contract — as a systems engineer — ha! And because I'd lost my IDs on the mugging and was no longer on cadet rules it seems it's valid — I don't have junior protection!! In other words I have to honour it though I was out of my brains when I signed. The captain's last words were, 'And may God have mercy on you' — WOW!!

BETADEN 10 *12.45.90*

They don't mess about!! Before morning call I was summarized, given a deep space kit and without further ado had to board a ship before sunrise. No countdown, nothing — we just blasted off. What have I got myself into? Passenger accommodation VERY basic and no question of wearing a suit. Food unattractive.

BETADEN 11 *23.67.90*

Bit wobbly in mind and body: over indulgence in 'things' I think — feel pretty uneasy, so what? VERY weird dream — a long passage with an open door at the end, bright light coming out. I stood just outside and could see the profile of quite a striking girl. She turned and looked at me — familiar — then I woke up . . .

BETADEN 16 57.72.90

Brief stopover during what seems to be an eternal series of hops between planets. Have almost lost interest in where I'm going due to general fatigue and unvarying monotony of shipboard life. Occasional change of ship but they're all the same really. Wonder if I'll be able to cope — and what about when I get there? I can't imagine what I claimed to have in the way of qualifications.

BETADEN 20   15.42.92

Feeling faintly disgusted. We're on some kind of colony called Starros or something like that. Its main function is as an interchange between several major interstellar ways and, to say the least, there are all sorts that populate the place. This afternoon, having found myself completely by accident in some sort of slave market, was really horrified to see girls pirated from convoys being sold off. They're obviously doped up to the eyeballs. They'll need to be. God only knows what lies ahead of them. You can hardly negotiate your rights with a letched-up Uranium. I find it all quite appalling but money is the name of the game here, so you are just another commodity.

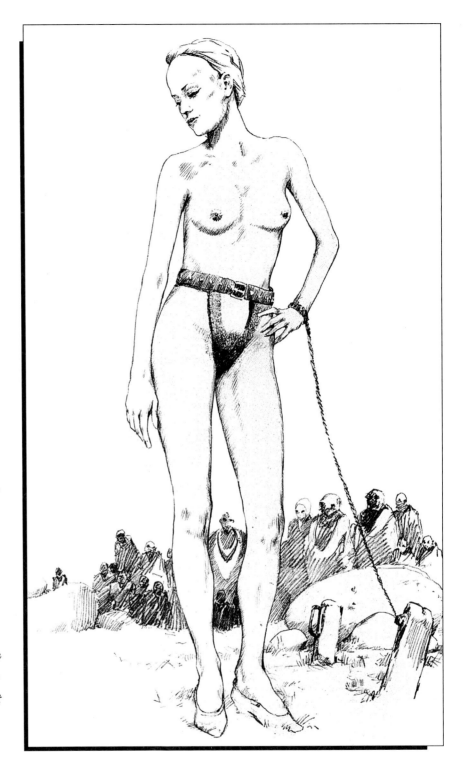

BETADEN 39   21.06.97

On the road again. No one will tell me exactly where we are going. There's no respect for any sort of human day condition so everyone, depending on their origin, makes their own routines. Sometimes I share cabins, sometimes I have the relative luxury of my own space. It's impossible to make friends — just as an acquantainceship is struck up another one falls at an interchange. Do I know who I am anymore?

Did I ever? Let's face it, with a routine like this you either live with it or sink. A few I've met are 'headstrong' but suprisingly few really. Strike, as always my constant ally, is amazingly difficult to get hold of. Maybe there's a serious future in marketing the stuff properly — if you could afford your own personal army.

23

BETADEN 50 *22.09.90*

Nightmares becoming increasingly frequent and — perhaps more worrying — more horrific. Past experiences blur and I find myself touching surfaces to see if they're hard or soft, cold or warm.

Some sixth sense tells me our destination is getting near. Today we have what I have been assured is the last interchange. No star configuration makes any sense this far out. I know I was going deep space but not this deep. It's amazing the pace at which civilization (?) is expanding.

Spent a pleasant hour on the bridge. The Nav took me through the galaxy — I'm ashamed to say I didn't know a single star.

BETADEN 51 *80.46.90*

I'm on the last ship to wherever. One every two light years I am told. It's huge. The biggest one yet. All company property now. Everyone, everything carries the company logo and you do it their way.

I'm no longer a straight passenger and have been put to work. Welcome relief and I feel my brain's beginning to warm up. Easy chores so far. VERY NERVOUS when I get put to serious work. Would love to see a copy of the contract — systems engineer can mean ANYTHING.

I at least now know my destination: Stasco 3, one of the biggest planets in this part of the sky, twice the size of Earth's sun and apparently very hostile outside — ho hum.

BETADEN 53　07.20.90

ARRIVAL, ARRIVAL!! Too exhausted to recount initial impressions except the most important, it's hot. GOD IT'S HOT! — more than 130 inside. Outside possibly 180 at the height of the suns. That is the other thing, Stasco 3 has ten suns. That partly explains the heat — I tried a few breaths outside and had to have medication for my lungs. New arrivals stay inside for the first quarter.

Because of the horrible environment we're all quartered in city blocks, about 10Ks high which travel on a vast track. The track is what Stasco is all about. The cities travel in relation to the suns and as they orbit Stasco so the structures move along the track. The relation is critical as the cities are TOTALLY dependent on solar energy. If a city stopped, all life would die within THREE hours. Movement on the track is paramount and I'm told there are actually explosives in the bogies to blow a city off in case of an actual break-down as at any time there are twenty cities on a given section of track.

BETADEN 54　20.19.90

I have the luxury of having today off to get acclimatized. I NEED IT. I've just discovered what I'm here as. Project engineer on the track! For God's sake, what do I know about structural work? The temperature variations on Stasco are so dramatic that the track is constantly fracturing. I'm being given a gang of five and we'll be working about 20Ks ahead of our city — Omega. We have to clear debris, repair breaks, weld rails, renovate embankments and possibly even bridges — all in at least 150 with 90% humidity and mainly hand tools!! Am BADGERING anyone for manuals.

BETADEN 62   19.41.20

Oberon, a really mild girl in our gang, has just been really beaten up by two of our meanest skips — they know we're all going down and so taking them with us. They're hopping mad. Pearl D is the senior and is a total bastard. She led the assault on Oberon. When I protested, three of her skips took me into a skoot and jerked me off — what hope have I got when even the skips take me.

46.08. Have got down to serious planning. I still have use of my personal skoot which has about 2000Ks range which is a lot. Downtrack less than an orbit back we passed a local logistics port. It doesn't have exit status. But if I jumped a carrier I could stow away, then transfer at its next dock — provided I could find an airzone plus food and water. Frankly, even dying in space would be better than this.

52.10. Got tipped through friendly sources — I daren't even mention their names — that I will go down at the end of orbit — probably for ten years. So that's it — I have to break within 20 days — I have absolutely no alternative.

61.05. My shuttle goes in for mid-term assessment in two days — good. It'll be in optimum condition.

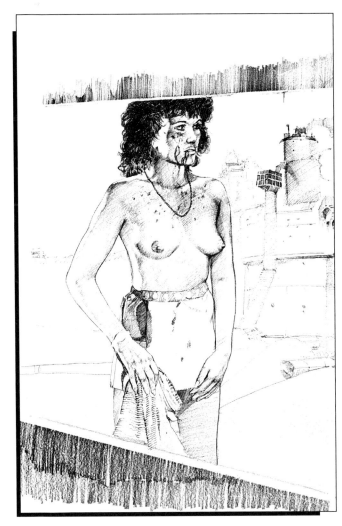

BETADEN 65   18.22.16

Pearl D is something of a legend. This is actually her THIRD tour — an unheard-of situation. She must be a total masochist. My crew are easily the most behind, almost an orbit and a half now (a record), so she was allocated to run our skips. She is also an absolute sadist and my bunch — no angels themselves — are genuinely terrified of her. At least she's straight. A rare event — and in all fairness I have to say she's halfway

Pearl D in action

reasonable till things get out of order — at which point she turns into a monster. This AM she knee-capped one of my girls who was resting due to heat exhaustion. With regard to my bunk, evading Pearl is my initial problem. She's recently started riding shotgun on the shuttle when I go on delivery runs — could she possibly anticipate my plans?

29

*Getting high — then dressed
for my scudder fight*

*Prisoner surveillance — you're
not left alone for a second*

*This is Sam — one of
the regular skips —
nicer than some*

BETADEN 72   06.14.59

*Still all very strange. Totally lost contact with Zed – don't
even know if she came up-country. I'm given far more
responsibility than I'm happy with. For example, this AM I
had to take the gang up the track 50Ks for ballasting and
lifting. Gravity is a little greater than Earth mean which
puts Omega on a loading of over 20,000 gross. Sunnyside
250 surface temperature can reach 200 in the SHADE. So,
bearing in mind the distortion the track is under, it's amazing
it holds up as well as it does. The work is much more manual
than I expected with prisoners frankly doing work a machine
could handle in seconds. So far there've been no track
breaks, but since the cities only pass each section once
every 3–5 years on the mountain sections it regularly
ruptures in the interval.*

*There's this insane pressure constantly to keep ahead
— the one thing that has been dinned into me is that under NO
circumstances can a city be stopped — obvious really. One
stopped city would hold up all the others — the suns would
pass out of reception — ergo one dead planet!*

*25.06. Despite the surveillance, discipline employee-wise is
very lax. The prison is a highly commercial undertaking —
provided no one escapes or dies. The guards (skips) can do
as they wish. At least strike is everywhere.*

BETADEN 76   02.19.97

In spite of the appalling conditions boredom is still a problem — off shift, I'm usually too tired to socialize. The skips keep to themselves, so apart from the gang I'm stuck mainly with engineering and maintenance folk. More out of curiosity than anything else I've joined the scudder league — the rules are as bizarre as the outfits and rituals. Both feet on the ground at all times and opponents must always be face to face right side to left side. Someone brought it from Tango Alpha where it forms a part of the native mating ritual. It should normally be fought male against female but I got out of that. Lost both my rounds on points — would have helped if I'd known what to do. Before and afterwards massive drinking ceremonies in outrageous outfits — got totally smashed and was put to bed.

25.86. Woke up and smoked a ball. Must have reacted with the hooch; started hallucinating like mad — incredible vision — was floating thru alien landscape in Grand Masters (top scudder division) outfit feeling totally disconnected and VERY erotic — extremely sensual sensations — not at all unpleasant but very vivid. Woke up to find I'd done this drawing whilst under the influence.

13.72. Saved by an angel in the gang. Lovely girl called Tess — was an engineer on Solus — a peer planet — she certainly knows her stuff. Have nabbed a heavy lifter and things are really moving — fishbolting as first tower breasts the horizon . . .

This was a strong girl — I lost!

All done up for the scudder coming out! The losers get tagged.

Flying — who knows where?

BETADEN 79 09.46.90

Classic example of why I have to get out of
here! The track blasts its way through
the Mid-Kalibor range, very mature
range of Alpine peaks. It utilizes one of
the major passes and Gohos (indigenous
natives and dropouts) have used its native
surface for a colony. After all, it takes
five of our years for the cities to
circumnavigate Stasco 3, so they don't
think in terms of our return. Anyway, I
turned up with the gang to work and we
had to clear them out. The head man didn't
want to know, said it was their land and all
the rest. I warned him that they wouldn't
mess about but they saw us off with a
couple of strings for our trouble. The
girls said let them get it but I made one more try and got
beaten up for my pains. So, in due course the familiar outline
of Omega breasted the horizon and bore down on the
shantytown. Nothing survived. Bodies, structures, the lot,
smeared downtrack for about 7Ks.

BETADEN 81 10.40.90

Still can't get over what happened at the pass. Am into a
very active planning phase. Can't say too much here — the
walls have eyes. Have made valuable contacts and subject to
transportation have a route in mind. In a quarter we'll be
near the only solid
city within the
hemisphere — Stos.
Will keep you posted.

Mesclin old town

BETADEN 90   11.29.91

Am using my skoot increasingly to foray. The idea is when I do the bunk, I'll start out as if on a trip to get the gear from my contacts and get going in earnest. Off to Mesclin to get a couple of outlaws — they used to work on Omega — who can help with the equipment. Payment could be a problem but basically I've a good strike stash due to the astute dealing and out country it's worth 20 times what you'd pay in a city. Basically I'm hoping to get out through an area called the Dagtal swamps. Thick turgid swamp with hidden mines just to make life interesting! Need a swamp buggy which is going to cost but have been given a few hints on how to keep the 'suppliers' happy.

Mesclin's a nasty little place full of very hostile alleys. My street plan is inaccurate and am currently LOST. Natives hostile. Expect some had relatives at the pass so you can hardly blame them. So far have traded jacket and vest for directions.

BETADEN 90   *18.29.91*

Bit of a hitch. Avoided nasty mugging I came across (stupid up-city tourist not staying with the flock). The attackers certainly had good noses and scented my strike bundle. Legged it but got jumped from a doorway!! Now no strike and a bit knocked around. Got held across a slab so they could have a bit of fun. Not very nice.

BETADEN 90   *22.29.91*

Not the best way to meet your contacts, battered, topless, and nothing to pay with. Well, they made the obvious suggestion and frankly I'm so desperate I took them up. So, three hot, sweaty and strenuous hours later I'm the proud temporary owner of a swamper. It's in good nick and I expect to stash it up at the ballast quarry where we're currently working. Loads of caves there so it should be easy.

BETADEN 90   *29.29.91*

Swamper stashed and ready to roll. Wish I could say the same of myself. Absolutely smashed. They certainly had their money's worth.

BETADEN 92   *29.40.91*

Fantastic opportunity. Had planned to break tomorrow after the gang went out on the last ballast run! However, blasting the last face we woke a rock monster. I'd heard of such beasts of course, but believe me, coming face to face with the real Mcoy is a salutary experience. Needless to say, total chaos all round. Those bastards weigh in at about 200 tons approx and two of them once turned a city over. They sleep inside the mountain partially trapped by cooling crust, and rarely move. Normally a hot fissure would give warning of their presence. They're cold blooded so don't show on sensors. Anyway, 1000 pounds of nitro had certainly woken this guy and he was not a happy person.

In the total confusion it was easy to get the swamper and now it's feet on the boards towards the badlands. It hasn't sunk in yet but, technically, for the first time in living memory I'm temporarily FREE FREE FREE!!

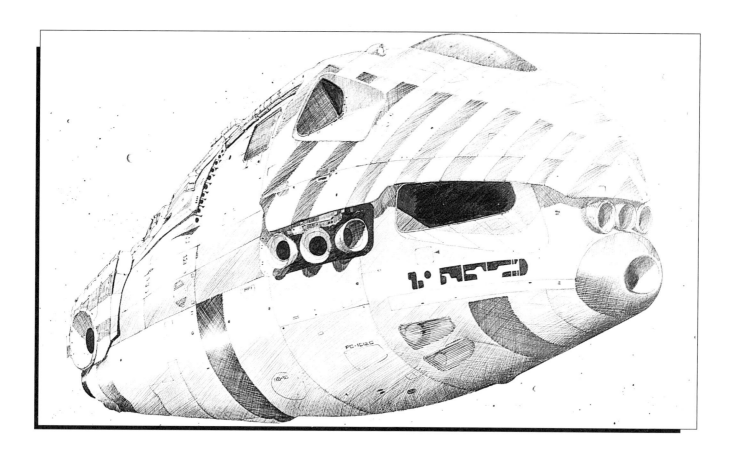

BETADEN 94   07.19.90

Fast moving stuff now. The swamp was terrifying — it's massively mined below the surface. They go off about one fathom down and if the explosion doesn't get you, you are either swamped by the gusher or drowned as the whorl fills. One of the reasons I gave those creeps in Mesclin such a good time was that they threw in a little device that activates the mine holds and makes them surface so you can see them — still alive and running.

BETADEN 95   40.19.90

Traded the swamper for a neat little flyer that can safely cruise a metre off the ground even over rocky terrain. So far have evaded everything because it's so manoeuvrable. I can run into canyons every time I see or sense a patrol. They're definitely out looking for me. Lots of low level activity.

68.19.90

Coming up for another tough section. Due to nearby patrols I am forced to run into an unknown side of the planet where the Mesclin folk said off-planet carriers make illicit stops. They didn't say why and I don't want to know, provided they'll take me. It means going to Kirren, a small satellite — the defences are weaker that way as theoretically it doesn't lead anywhere.

BETADEN 96   02.10.90

Lost precious fuel avoiding tower robots — couldn't believe how quickly they could move. They behave as if swatting flies and can certainly outrun this heap at ground level. In the end needed long burn to gain safe altitude — one more burn will get me out of gravitational pull but leave next to nothing for manoeuvring.

109.60.90

Burn successful. I am in orbit and have picked up outer marker for Kirren. It looks very decayed and signal weak. Am drifting badly but dare not burn 'till in sight of the drome.

110.62.90

Master signal gone. No landing beacon. Actually I'm lost. Enough air for half a day. Enough fuel for landing and that's it. If Kirren has gravity I've had it. Desperately scanning for beacon.

BETADEN 97   *20.49.90*

Made it! Beacon showed at last possible moment. Very weak even when I was on the ground. Drome deserted, buildings derelict. Went outside to investigate and got grabbed by A PLANT!! Very traumatic, it seemed to know what it was doing. I certainly knew what it was doing. Used a sting and after two burns it desisted. Two hours later a cargoliner landed as if it was the norm and the crew didn't bat an eyelid when a very dishevelled I enrolled as a passenger to Storren.

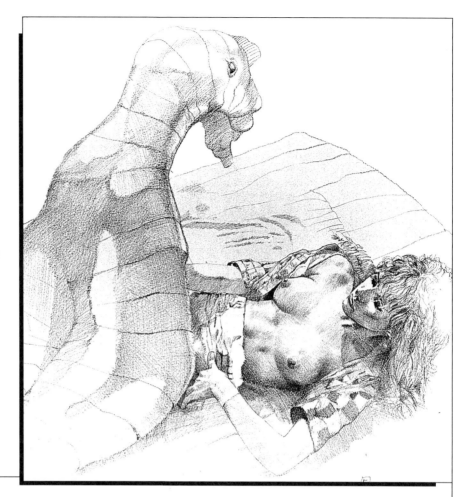

10.52.90

One really loses track of time, apart from the fact the ship's still on BB time — really, time is meaningless. Outside it's just black, black, black. From the dome, of course, I can watch the stars, but needless to say there's no sense of movement. We're on stopover Agate 10 — so named for the profusion of precious stones it generates. Going down it was funny to see the ship from the outside. After all these orbits — even though we've travelled less than 3 light years — you begin to think there is no outside. I've come down with two juniors. They're silly and good fun.

12.52. Quite surprised. From above Storren the main city looked so beautiful with all the twinkling lights and glittering towers. Actually the streets are filthy. There's not much traffic, and the buildings are very run down. Many are empty.

12.96. We have to explore on foot. The teenies were expecting to buy souvenirs. Where do they get their money from? But what shops there are are mainly for basics — and poor quality at that.

14.02. We've been told to keep in groups. I can see why. Huddled in doorways are very down-and-out characters — many aliens. After my recent experience I dare not have a foray. I'd hoped to bunk off and find some strike with my few remaining dinos — assuming that's the currency here. Desperate to break away for a hunt.

19.06. Everything happens to me: saw three halfway decent humans. Managed to shuffle off and explain my problem. They just laughed and said I could get a real ball for the dinos I'd got. Had to risk them being straight. They said money up front and meet you at the terminal before you go back up. I honestly thought they were good guys. Needless to say, hung around 'till the last shuttle — no people — no dope — now no money.

23.90. Things go from disaster to Armageddon. Tonight they have two other girls in the cabin. Hung out in the dome 'till the shakes became impossible.

BETADEN 100 20.55.90

Last day of the quarter. Normally I'd be in a good mood, especially as Deltaday is my birth quarter, but we're still stuck at Storren. Technical problems, reasonable enough but it doesn't help my paranoia. What's more, it's heavily patrolled and at any time I could be asked for my bracelet and then the cat would be out of the bag. On top of that one of the juniors got busted, no reason, nothing. We were playing scat for low breaks when security walked in and just picked her up. She didn't look surprised and trotted off

with them. God, they're so innocent and I feel frustrated because I would have intervened but then they'd have wanted my ID and that would have been that.

48.96.70

Quite a lot of kids in this place. All on the hustle! Tough but nice to me. Had some strike free — sort of — charge up an alley with a gang of them. They're certainly born survivors. Apparently the reason for the delay is there's some sort of war here and they're expecting a raid.

DELTADEN 02 20.91.90

There certainly is a war on. Awoken at dawn with the most massive bombardment. And guess what, the spaceport is the prime target!!

22.91.90

The spaceport is burnt to a cinder. There are about 20 ships over the city with shuttles rising and descending like flies. Plenty of gunfire, shouting, screaming, looting. Buildings burning — it's almost not a novelty.

24.91.90

Perhaps stupidly, decided to see what the situation was. Total chaos. Naturally am desperate to take a ship but even if one could get off, the hardwear about is formidable.

29.91.90

Met up with a group who seem to know what they're about — there appears to be an outlying field that so far has escaped from too much attention. We're running for that in a group of vehicles through street riddled with gunfire. No more time to write, the book just almost stopped a bullet!!

DELTADEN 04 01.70.91

I think I still have a sense of humour. We did make a ship — a company ship sent in especially for refugees!! No time to check IDs of course. Better still we were heading for the Quator Galaxy more than 2000 light years back home!! All at no charge to yours truly. Was actually beginning to think of searching for supplies, food and a warm bunk in that order, of course, when we were attacked. Our ship was just a carrier so we didn't stand a chance. After running for almost a light year the captain had to agree to heave to or be blown to pieces. A very unpleasant group of characters came aboard. Frankly my skin crawled. Anyone they thought would be useful was taken off and the rest left on board. It's some sort of drug war or something (ho hum) and when we were taken off they just blew the carrier up. I've seen some things, but to callously destroy innocent lives makes me choke.

DELTADEN 06 *90.17.90*

This lot are nothing more than a bunch of pirates, no morals, scruples, nothing. They live and die by the gun. It's a massive fleet and apparently the company is one of their favourite targets. So much so that now there's an all out war raging.

After hitting, stripping and grabbing as much as they could, we are being taken well into deep space. Am very nervous. We're just a commodity and my mind runs back to the slave girls in the market. The bands are dividing into groups and basically we're traded as currency. There are a few humans in my lot but looking at the state of their 'possessions' it's not hard to imagine what sort of fate awaits me. Life on Stasco 3 is beginning to seem positively harmonious.

DELTADEN 10   06.20.90

It's amazing how one becomes used to routines. Especially if you accept your lot. Some of my 'gang' are actually quite interesting if you're prepared to discount their disgusting appearance. The law on board is that the weaker give way to the tougher, so being a practical sort of person I've gone in with the meanest bunch I can find and have sort of become accepted as a person rather than a possession. There is a price to pay but at least it means that my life is no longer totally in the balance. And tomorrow is always another day.

20.44.90

As far as I can gather we're heading for their base. It's really tucked off any course and it's well nigh impossible to sense in deep space. Their gear is in a hopeless state and I've actually become rather useful to them. So much so that I've managed to lose my valuable 'prisoner' status and am genuinely accepted as a groupie.

DELTADEN 11   21.56.90

Had time to do a nice drawing of myself. When I look at the first pages, how I've changed! Anyway I'm all fitted in the relevant gear and am looking forward to my new home.

18.96.90

Actually took part in a raid and rather enjoyed it. It's quite fun to see fear in the eyes of a fat cat and since this one worked for the company I can say I got great pleasure in helping work the sod over. What's more you get to keep what you take. Have a couple of nice bits of jewellery.

30.59.90

Have just caught sight of the base — it's beautiful!! A white series of asteroids with tower cities spread all over them. It doesn't have a name apparently. I find the local aliens still a bit disgusting but I don't notice the general smell of bad breath and bodies anymore.

DELTADEN 14   60.91.90

A few impressions of life around here. Since these guys create the strike — there are massive tanks of it above the city docks — it's lying around the place for anyone to use, anytime, anyway. At first I just couldn't believe it and am ashamed to say was only semi-conscious for a couple of days. Just as well I am still treated in some ways as a possession, if you know what I mean. For instance, there was a massive celebration when the fleet got back and basically anyone who was in the mood had you or you got your head blown off. Have managed to create a certain amount of group allegiance so that sort of situation will not arise so often now. In fact

I'm now getting the chance to use a little authority, so much so that up to a point I have a small but useful bunch of followers.

DELTADEN 15   70.96.28

We have a particularly annoying and stupid character in our group called Yascar. He's a rock gopher, so incredibly pea-brained. His idea of fun is to chuck rocks at your head which naturally he is able to do with incredible speed and accuracy. This morning he caught me a real cracker — so one of these days as far as I am concerned he's destined for the cooking pot.

DELTADEN 20   31.06.90

Had a battleaxe fight with an Amazon from our main rival group. Had to be stopped when I almost took her arm off. Apparently she's very good at time locks and suchlike so they'd rather she kept her arm. Thought I did well.

DELTADEN 21   06.90.90

Plans are well afoot for a big convoy raid. There's a juicy one coming through the Antares passage next quarter so everyone is making a real big effort to get on with each other. Because of my incredibly good ship control (!!!) I've been doing some piloting on meteorite raids. These are rather fun. It involves getting under the screens and skimming towards the craters no more than a metre above the surface — grabbing the rock and getting out before guns or worse can be trained on you. So far my nose for good rocks has worked well so I'm increasingly flavour of the month. In fact I reckon I shall be running my own group before long.

DELTADEN 22   06.09.90

Really satisfying bust today, and I was in the hot seat! We were returning from a fairly hairy meteor run and I was a bit worried about the quality of the rock. We were actually scanning shipboard for tail chasers and by sheer good luck picked up a liner all on its sweet lonesome. I took part in the boarding and have snaffled for personal sale or worse (!) two very nice hostesses. There's a big market on Stos next quarter so I can either rent them out or keep them A1 clean for the auction. Our group made top money this quarter so there's some strong rivalry brewing.

DELTADEN 26   01.90.90

Sleeping really badly. Have been getting increasing stomach pains for some time now but daren't let on. I'm really in with the chance of group leader — no one's made them more money and we've had fewer shoot-outs than any other group — and any sort of stupid female problem would really blow the plug. Plenty of strike would be the old remedy but I need to keep my head clear as my piloting and shooting is the best in our section.

DELTADEN 27   02.86.90

Very exciting. The convoy job is on and our bid for lead attack was accepted. That means we get 10% more than anyone else of the share — that's because we open the can. These damn pains don't help — they're not getting any better and my stomach is definitely swelling — clothes aren't fitting. I know I'm not imagining it.

DELTADEN 29   01.07.90

This is it. We're off first call carrying every armament the ships will take. We're not expecting too much resistance as they think no one knows they're using the passage. He he! If I make as much as I think I will on this I will be able to flog the hostesses and put my feet up for a bit. Stomach more settled, thank God.

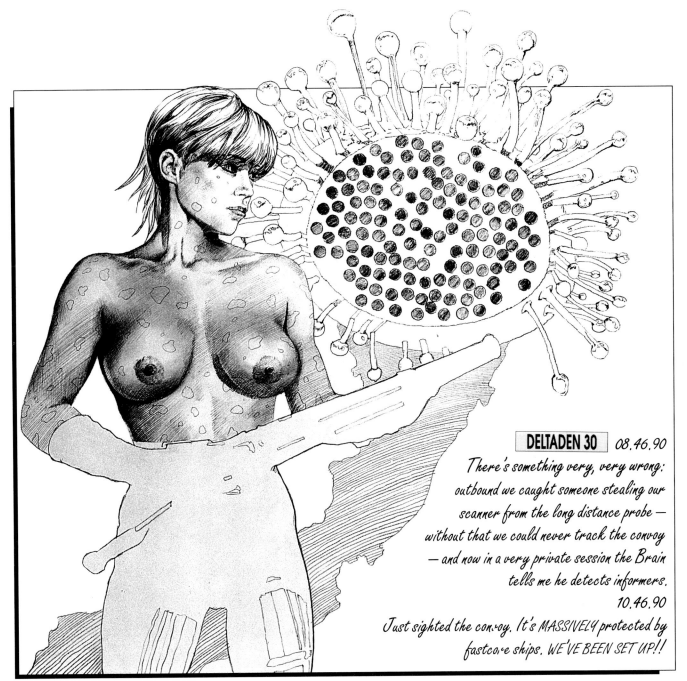

DELTADEN 30 08.46.90

There's something very, very wrong: outbound we caught someone stealing our scanner from the long distance probe — without that we could never track the convoy — and now in a very private session the Brain tells me he detects informers.

10.46.90

Just sighted the convoy. It's MASSIVELY protected by fastcore ships. WE'VE BEEN SET UP!!

DELTADEN 30   12.18.60

Why is it when I'm on my feet after all my trials and tribulations I'm always knocked over again? LIFE WAS GOING SO WELL!! I should have been more suspicious.

14.18.60

We've been well and truly set up. It was a total trap. The tankers and transports are clearly empty and there's ordinance coming at us like angry wasps on a bonfire. Needless to say we can hardly stand and fight but no one's got a ship that can outrun a core! It's going to be a massacre and frankly I think it's a bloody shame.

DELTADEN 30   18.18.60

Stomach going mad, at a time like this! It's as if there's something in there shitting itself — which, bearing in mind everyone else is, would not surprise me.

20.18.60

We've taken several hits and have small but so far controllable fires. The stuff is coming at us from all sides and we just don't have the sort of sophisticated screens to control the situation. I'm proud of our guys — they're hitting back with everything they've got and at least we'll go down in style.

DELTADEN 30   25.18.60

Just caught sight of Nemo's ship going up, a crewman just clinging to wreckage. For a second our eyes met — he was still alive — then he was gone, a puff of red running down the stylex.

40.18.60

We're running absolutely flat out. There's so much debris flying around the cores can't come in too close. By keeping a couple of carcasses between us and them and building up the drive I'm chancing the barrier. On paper the frame won't take it but since we're due for a missile up the bum any second, what is the choice?

DELTADEN 30   45.18.90

The reactor's white hot, we're pumping lead and my stomach has definitely got something inside it!! From where, for God's sake — humans are not supposed to be able to be fertilized by aliens.

48.18.90

WE GOT A CORE!!! Direct hit possibly down a tube but the effect was the same. One moment he was coming at us, firing death, the next a big beautiful rosy glow! We're almost up to light speed and if the frame holds we should bang through any second now.

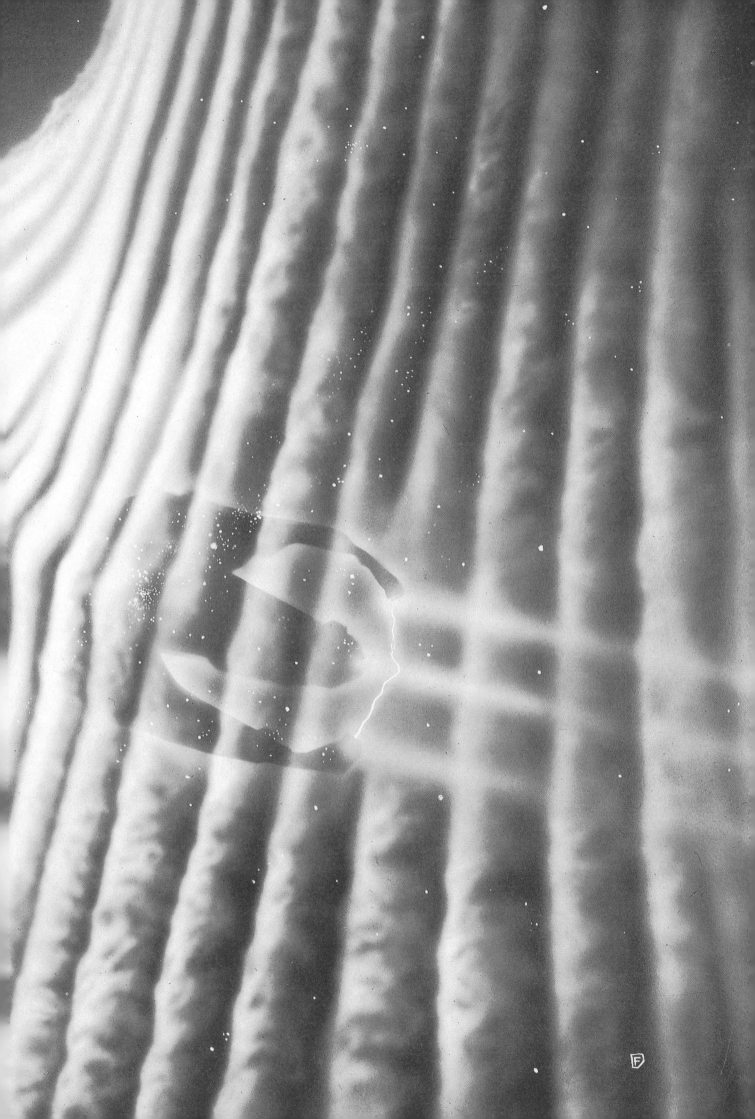

DELTADEN 31   90.47.90

We made it back to base, despite not being able to hold post-light for more than 50,000 light years. Debris everywhere on the way back. It's been one hell of a battle and I don't know what our chances are of regrouping.

01.50.90

A sad and serious meeting with Kol. He acts between Brain and the rest. He told me our ship was one of the few to survive and they've picked up a massive fleet on its way. It's surely the battle fleet and we're done for. I'm all for going down fighting, but rather kindly he told me I was still a young woman and had a full life ahead of me. He said if I took a lifeboat I certainly wouldn't be noticed in the confusion — so that's what I'm going to do.

DELTADEN 32   81.08.90

Felt terrible. I really mean that. A true rat for leaving a sinking ship. I know that when I first came out I was treated as they would any female (human) booty, but in time I earned their respect through true, and although I say it myself, talented endeavour. For a small moment in time I belonged somewhere.

The end was frighteningly quick. The attacking fleet was massive. There were a lot of company ships in there so that is one big, big score to settle. The asteroids put up a spirited defence but they didn't stand a chance. I took one of our lifeboats filled to the brim with goodies and got out of the hold before the rockets went up. Actually from where I was watching it all looked rather beautiful.

DELTADEN 56   10.82.90

What annoys me about that cluster of grey cells laughingly known as my brain is that the wretched things put an idea together — all of their own accord — plant it and watch it grow whilst they sit back to see how I'll deal with their maturing creation.

So here I am sitting in this plastic blob, vaguely staring at star charts and calculating fuel against distance, and suddenly with appalling clarity an idea has gelled and hit me with almost physical force. The reason I'm in this position is basically that I would not tolerate the life of a dodo and have always wanted to go to Earth. It's so simple, it is after all the spiritual home of my race — even if we're only allowed there in old age. I simply wanted to cut a few corners so I signed that damn contract spurred on by that incredible book and a gut full of hooch.

Ergo: I want to go Earth. I am ethnically an Earth Person — so I shall go to Earth. I appreciate it is forbidden and the place is supposed to be heavily defended but quite frankly after what I've been through it should be a piece of piss. I should have enough air and fuel for 10,000 light years so I shall take a break, examine my curiously inflated navel (WHAT IS THAT IN THERE!), and do a portrait.

DELTADEN 62   71.10.90

The mystery of the expanding tummy was rather abruptly solved this morning. I woke up to find a thingy looking at me from the end of the bunk. I just don't know what my feelings are. At last I have my insides back and I can truly say a great weight is off my mind. Frankly it's been as near as anyone my age is going to come to an immaculate conception. The little sod hopped out when I was sleeping and has even licked up all the slop — well, almost all — and nasty bits that must have come out with him.

I say he, but looking at him he couldn't possibly be female, could he? He's sort of clucking and chirping — rather sweet really — but his overall green tone is not to my taste. I'm certainly not going to breast feed him.

DELTADEN 63   18.92.90

Had a rummage through past entries of the book. After all, even things must have a dad. Calculating days of incubation is no good — my guts started playing up about the time I became group leader. Possible fertilization points would have been when that gang of drop-outs banged me after ripping me off for the strike — or when I paid for the swamper — that was a very heavy session and several aliens were a very green colour. On the other hand there were some heavy sessions when the pirates took me. But the funny thing is the event that seems significant is when that plant jumped me. It had a very thorough little bang. The thing is, it was bright purple and the thingy is sort of grey-green. Perhaps his colour will change as he matures. So for the time being he's Son of Purple. SOP to you book.

Another clue — there was no plastic on that station as far as I could see, so that's probably why it was abandoned. SOP absolutely belts through the stuff. IN FACT IT'S ALL HE EATS, which is becoming a problem because this thing is made of the stuff and unless I put down soon there will be nothing to put down.

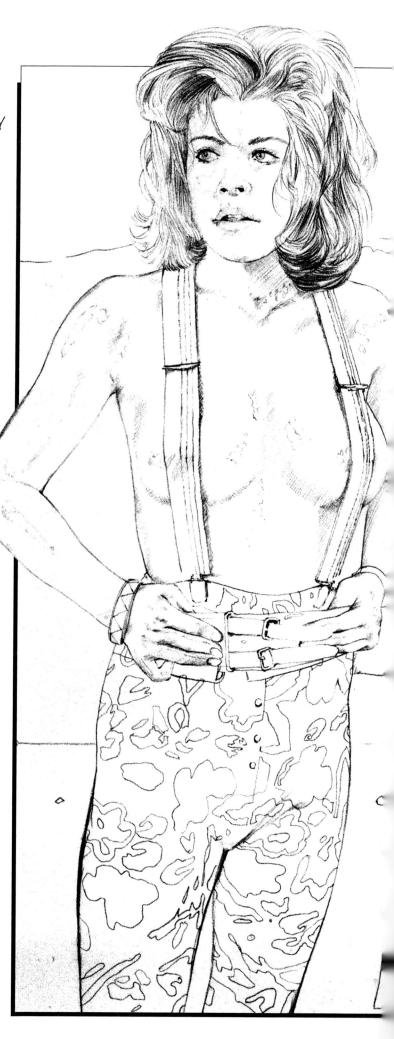

DELTADEN 75   18.62.90

This is what's known as resource innovation. I managed to get a little further down when SOP ate me out of house and home. He's incredibly self-sufficient and if he wasn't quite so revolting I could feel almost maternal towards him. Anyway, as soon as we hit terra firma he massacred a nearby freighter, causing rather a commotion. I had to do a runner. SOP is growing by the MINUTE, and as far as I can calculate is doubling in size every demi-quarter — his appetite for plastic is stupendous.

DELTADEN 76   21.46.90

The ship has made it to a no-hopers colony on Quandor, a satellite in the Arch Galaxy. Just another crossroads really and I've been been forced to do a little hustling to keep body and soul together. Met of all people one of the juniors I saw getting busted on whatever it was called, the memory blurs. Her route here was as obscure as mine and she put me up to this work. Mainly humans so we hope. We've decided to either hustle a shuttle crew and pinch the ship — or possibly do a short-term rental and not come back. Back on the strike with a vengeance — you need it to cope with the work — so income in is slightly less than income out — a familiar tale.

DELTADEN 79   23.14.90

Doing a session with junior and a fairly dopey shuttle crew. Good clean boys so at some stage should be no problem in getting the ship.

DELTADEN 80   71.10.90

Blew junior out. She got greedy and wanted too much of the action. I got her to do a scene with the shuttle crew at a greenhouse (more of a turn on among all those leaves and pooh!) rather than shipboard. While all six of them were living out their wildest fantasies nipped back to the ship and with a neat bit of re-wiring got myself airborne. So we are back in business folks. No sign of SOP but that character is a born survivor — anyway, how could I get 10 metres of beastie in a ship this size? Plenty of fuel and supplies, so it's heigh ho for a burn back to civilization.

DELTADEN 82   70.21.90

Many things have happened to me since this book began. I've been shot at, captured, sold, raped, manipulated and given birth — but above all else I survived. Now, however, this is a really different thing — THIS IS VERY DIFFERENT. I was forced to keep low to evade pursuit and got myself tangled in a very devious mountain chain. Canyon led to canyon and stupidly I cut through a natural arch to avoid climbing and showing on the scanners. Unfortunately it was a real blind alley and at over 500Ks I burst through into this lake surrounded by cliffs. There wasn't enough time to climb and the after burner was playing up so I deliberately stalled down into the water. No undue problem — I've handled worse

when we were nicking meteorites. I figured on sitting tight until the fans cooled and I could clean out the burners. In fact it was delightfully peaceful and I sat with the hatch open smoking a spliff and watching the starlight on the water. In the gloom, I became aware that there was some sort of watchtower at one end of the lake. Obviously left over from the wars. Suddenly its head went down to scan the surface and within seconds the biggest set of claws I've seen in my life came bursting up. Total panic on board!! Sod the barrier. I revved up for emergency blast off but with reduced power had a job to gain height. One pair of claws got me, taking out the motors and the main fuel tank.

DELTADEN 83 *01.06.90*

Still shaking from yesterday's experiences. When the claws got the ship I thought I was done for. The damage was massive but somehow I stayed airborne. Just as well, the whole area was a mechanical wasteland. Someone hadn't told the machines the war was over. Whole tracts of landscape had been quagmired by fighting machines grappling with each other, clawing each other to bits — smashing the pieces with the sort of venom you expect from living persons. The best of it was other machines would then come running along to pick up the pieces and reconstruct the things. Then the whole ghastly business would begin again.

My surviving motor kept blipping and blupping and I was losing horrendous amounts of fuel but somehow I stayed aloft. Fortunately I could raise myself thru thermals and this gave some uplift, but it was obvious the ship was done for — after all I went thru to get my hands on it! I'm beginning to seriously think there's a celestial joker — some omnipotent being who looks at us funny little characters and whenever we pick ourselves up gives another nudge to see what will happen then. Well, whoever he is he's got a real surprise coming — because make it to Earth I shall!

20.19.90

This thing has had it. I could probably patch it up given adequate facilities but the computing is totally foreign so everything has to be on manual. Fatigue a real problem. Haven't slept for two days. The landscape's evened out a bit and we're over a very hot desert. Will utilize thermals for height and try and get a starfix. If I ground I'm dead! Either from heat or more of those damned machines.

36.19.90

Heat intense. Can feel it thru the canopy which is triple thickness glaze. Turbulence now a problem. Am definitely approaching a very hostile atmosphere. Even if the motor lasts we might break up!

DELTADEN 83   06.54.90

And this is my birth quarter!!! Heat is formidable — frame buckling and creaking in every direction — motor very much on its last legs!!! Ground temperature possibly above 200, so if we go down *THAT IS IT*.

06.58.90

Just banged up about 2Ks by a vicious thermal — literally a solid wall of atmosphere. Cab seals beginning to blow. But for the heat would try a suit, if I dared leave the controls. Can get a good view from here — we're going over a volcano!! *A BIG ONE*. We must be almost over the cone.

06.90.90

Just sent up another few Ks. She won't take much more of this. Heat impossible. If I faint we're done for.

07.18.46

Some cooling — is that possible — am frantically trying to remember what they tried to din into me about volcano micro-climates. Downside a very strong suction draught if I remember . . . very hard to think . . . can't take much more of this . . . am tempted to try and set the auto . . . if only I could understand the numeration . . . going for it anyway . . . just . . . just too much . . .

DELTADEN 83   07.68.90

Wonderful sense of achievement — the Joker — *HE DOES EXIST!* — set me a task and I pulled it. Much cooler now and I've got plenty of height. Passed out for a while but must have cracked the auto setting. About two light years of fuel then it's glide path to whatever with a few drops in hand for ground approach. Turbulence marginal and decreasing, must be over the worst.

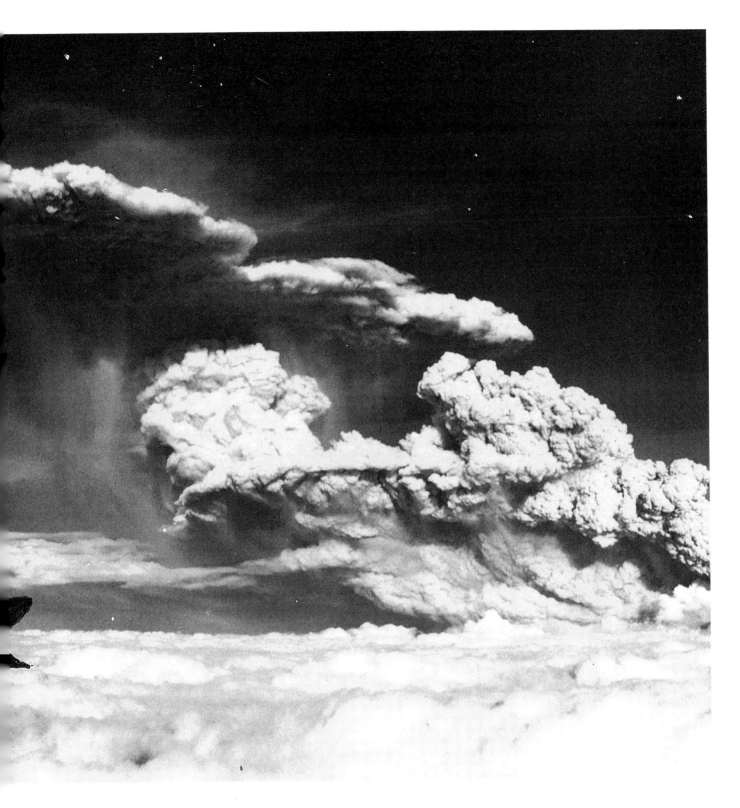

DELTADEN 83   *08.14.90*

On glide now. Motor died a while ago. Total peace and serenity. It's all out of my hands. Feel no fear.

08.18.90

THE MOST FANTASTIC SIGHT!!! REALLY DO NOT BELIEVE MY EYES. Looking back to check my rate of descent was marvelling at the ash cloud thrown up by this Vesuvius —

very dramatic— and there, bobbing in the cloud stands Son of Purple. The little sod!!! Either he's now the size of a mountain (some mountain!) or he's riding the jet stream. In any event he's as happy as a skylark. Wonder if he can see me. His ugly mug (GOD IT'S UGLY) is splitting a huge grin and he's bobbing and ducking as if the whole thing is a game!

DELTADEN 83   20.56.90

Thru the cloud-base I could see some sort of lighting but with half the instrumentation dead had no way of checking it out. Didn't dare call in and anyway was now committed on my glide-path. The main worry was that I was over a city and would end up impaling myself on a tower block.

In the event, below base I could see a clear and mercifully still landscape. I gave the motor its last chance and the dear thing responded with a final burn. In a run that the academy would have been proud of I made a turn towards a really massive structure that was the sole artificial feature in an otherwise very rocky terrain. Touchdown was textbook and there I was.

Almost symbolically the hatch fell off before I could test the atmosphere and I found myself breathing the most incredibly pure air. Terrific feeling of homecoming. Perhaps this was the Joker's palace?

27.18.90

What looked from a distance a huge structure is in fact as big as a world! Because its face is featureless there is no sense of scale. I thought I was a matter of metres away when I landed. In fact it's taken almost a day to get to its base, a distance of some 20Ks. The wall has no obvious aperture. I did another 10 Ks along one side then quite unexpectedly found an aperture. Entering, I found a long corridor. Strange sense of familiarity?

32.20.90

Very, very tired. Technically I'm long past bedtime but in here there is constant light. I have a beautiful sky above me, and a volcano — surely not the same one — in the distance. Following the sound of running water, I've come to a strange monolith with water — pure — beautiful — (EARTH WATER?) cascading from its pores. Was about to go for a swim when a ship came up the valley and hovered as if watching me. Am hiding 'till I can work out whatever's going on. Don't feel frightened — just puzzled.

DELTADEN 84   16.91.90

Must have slept for ages. It's a land of volcanoes, but sleeping ones. Somnolent, not menacing, and all this must be inside the structure. Who built all this? Something very strange that I cannot for the moment put my finger on.

Have travelled for some time through a warm, wet, but above all comfortable forest. Delicious fruits. It's as if all my problems are over. Am seriously beginning to wonder if somehow I've broken thru to EARTH. Some sort of back door or something — but technically I'm galaxies away — by my estimate a two-light year journey.

It's the water that gets me — and the volcanoes. The one that almost killed me was big — very very big — but these ones are old — not gigantic — and a fresh wind blows their vapours away. A hunch tells me it's worth searching for people.

DELTADEN 85 *20.19.90*

I found people alright. I came over the brow of a hill and found the most delightful port spread below me. A deep blue sea that made you want to jump into it. And languid ships — strangely powered — silent — gliding over the surface. And again the volcanoes that would imply a young landscape but this is obviously a very old one. There's nothing to lose so I'm going down. Wonder if you need money here?

DELTADEN 85 *14.56.90*

I've walked for possibly half a day now. Can't understand a word people are saying and somehow the clothes look from another time. Why should this place be in the same time as elsewhere? No one accosts me, asks me my business — they don't even appear to notice me. Feel totally nonplussed. The environment is so fresh — so pure — but the people and town so artificial. If only I could crack the language . . .

DELTADEN 86   *40.51.90*

Feeling a bit better. Have encountered my first bit of violence. In fact behind the scenes there's quite a lot going on here. Going up from the quayside the pleasant, almost classical buildings gave way to more sombre structures. Then the outlines of more familiar ghetto towers appeared. Right in the middle of some waste ground a gang fight was going on. Mean machinery. Probably a drag near so I should be able to score. Then further on some flying guys were jumping a merchant's house. Quite a lot of grief! Felt like joining in. Wouldn't mind a bit of rape and pillage — seems more my forte.

There are quite a few flyers around. Think I'll check them out since they seem to run things around here!

DELTADEN 87   *14.82.90*

Got a ride from a flyer. We didn't actually converse but both seemed to know what the other wanted. My experience with the pirates probably helped. The flyers sit out in towers up country. Air not so good here — bit fetid and musty but they certainly generate the action.

The post — Affron — is quite a rich trading post run by an enclave of merchants. It's a close community and outside of their affairs they don't want to know.

The flyers have lived off them for generations. Providing they don't take too much, the merchants can live with it — also it means the merchants stay in business and there's more for everyone. No merchants and the flyers would die. Should have used those principles on the gang!

GAMMADEN 02 20.36.90

Survival rears its ugly head. Going in with the flyers had one obvious problem — I can't fly and slightly galling from my point of view — they regard people without wings as a bit second class. So, unfortunately, for a time I've got to attempt to earn an honest living as this place appears to have well-organized but low-key crime. Anyway, being busted in a place like this would mean being confined to boredom more than anything else.

One strange thing: I came into a gigantic building or structure — call it what you want — and here is this world. Every time I say to someone why is this world *INSIDE* they change the subject or move on. It's so bizarre — there's a sun, wind, even a couple of moons — but it all feels so artificial.

Am temporarily working on a fuel terminal for a couple of the local fat cats — this way I can check out ship movements and plan my next move.

GAMMADEN 05 40.02.90

Gave the terminal up. Money was lousy and couldn't smoke (anything) on duty. Anyway — there were hardly any ship movements. It's like this place is really a dream world. I really am beginning to think in terms of 'inside and outside'.

Anyway — think this is the Joker's palace and one day I'll just meet him walking down the road. He'll probably say something stupid like — 'Hello, J. And how are you enjoying your time with us?' I've even begun to think — what is he expecting me to do now — is this paranoid? Anyway — I'm working at a breakers. Really, it's the robots doing the work but my main aim is to scavenge gear. Getting out of this place is beginning to be a real problem. At the same time I can't help being curious — how big is this building?

Most of the material coming in is obviously from a war that's currently happening — I saw a head fall out of a ship's carcass the other day — so that means there's some action going on somewhere.

GAMMADEN 20 14.20.90

After what seems in retrospect to have been a period of total monotony, decided to really seriously consider my next move. Getting a ship — or even a ride — seems to be a non-existent possibility. The place is just not transportation orientated. Everyone is so damned content — they all have their role in society and are happy to go thru the motions.

Have taken a hostess job at a nightclub in the hope of coming across a flight crew. So far the clientele appears to be fat happy merchants and bankers — haven't even had my bottom pinched yet. Much more of this and steam will be coming out of my ears.

Quite a lot of ships coming into the yard now with useful bits on but so far no useful frames. Glad the robots do the work. There are often bits of body wedged in nooks and crannies. From the state of them they haven't been long dead, so maybe the war's not too far away.

GAMMADEN 22 18.50.90

Amazing event in my dreary little existence! Saw what appeared to be a familiar face at the club last night. After a while had a chance to talk — it was Zoe — the kid I was hustling with when I was trying to get out of Quandor.

She looked a bit perkier than the last time I saw her — and here's a new turn — she's doing well selling aliens on the slave market up country — I didn't know there WAS one in this sugar-coated land. She reckons there's a good chance to do dealing on a sister planet called Mercon. It's all such an eye-opener. Here I've been sucked into this womb-like existence and all the time the big outside world's been plugging along! AND she had a fistful of strike. What an evening. We're going up country next quarter-day together.

GAMMADEN 23 *89.40.90*

Good market — well worth checking out. Did some neat dealing — girls quite good quality. Apparently there's a big war happening between Treens and Zirdans in this galaxy. Plenty of useful fall-out. If only I can get up that way could certainly pick up something useful — either a ride or, even better, my own ship.

Am beginning to wonder about Son of Purple as well. There was that wonderful moment when I saw him in the

clouds and since then nothing. If he's anything like the size I imagined him to be info should have filtered through to even this quiet little corner.

Have decided to finish in the yard soon while I'm still in funds and go walkabout. Should perhaps work the market a bit — I turned those girls around the same day — then when I've built up a good stash try and buy my way along the line. Must check this 'building' out sometime.

GAMMADEN 25   02.15.89

Been working the market quite successfully. Girls very
good quality. There are some big convoys that have gone
down and am getting very impatient to get up that way. At
the moment it's really costing me to buy them in. Am
thinking of going in with a gang and doing our own raids.

Through Zoe have met a very interesting bunch! They
use robots to bust into settlements — nothing can stop them
so there's no damage to the raiders even if the settlers are
well armed. You get the robots off one of the other convoys
— they need cash so will sell surplus quite cheaply.

40.16.89

Have made up my mind for sure. As of tomorrow I go
walkabout. Phase one — check out this world-in-a-building
— it really nibbles at me and until I beat this Mr Joker
paranoia I can't really operate successfully. Zoe thinks it's
a strange obsession to say the least. She actually laughed
and said how could you have a whole world in a building, and

swears she's been here eons — flies, travels around but
sees nothing unusual.

58.25.89

Am now fully finished and paid up from the yard. Have some
very useful kit. No one has seen or heard rumours re. Son
of Purple — very strange.

60.46.89

Very excited. Have said what few farewells are necessary.
Am going walkabout toute seule to begin with but will
rendezvous at the market with Zoe and friends in a few days
time — once I've got this thing out of my system.

Don't really have any amazing plans in mind — just go
out and about and check things out. After all, if I find one of
the walls all I've got to do is keep following it.
Theoretically, if I travelled long enough I should get back
to where I started. Zoe says (her last word on the
subject) if this place has walls why hasn't she herself
flown into them?

GAMMADEN 26   08.19.89

Zoe's lent me her ground flyer which helps. It's slow — cumbersome — but is definitely better than travelling on foot. The terrain changes quite quickly and not having any maps or navigation grids doesn't help.

10.20.89

Can't shake this strange feeling of familiarity — I suppose it's why I've decided on this crazy trip. I now believe in the Joker and I'm convinced he knows all about me — I feel I'm almost his personal toy — sets me up — knocks me down — then sees how I'll react to the next obstacle.

49.14.89

Country now getting very weird — not the sort of terrain I've ever encountered before. Overnight stop going to be a problem. I'll sleep well and anything could come upon me. The flyer won't stay hovering without manual control so I'm obliged to stay grounded overnight if I want to rest. No sensors or perimeter lasers or anything sophisticated like that. Well, I've survived so far — familiar line!

GAMMADEN 27   20.19.89

Woke up in the middle of the night in a cold sweat. Low, bright moonlight highlighting strange and bulbous plants. Were they as close as that when I went to sleep? Just couldn't relax. Lay with my back to a tree and just watched the landscape.

The trouble with moonlight is that you can imagine anything in the shadows. Vivid memories of my treatment at the hands of Purple came flooding in. Just can't help it. If only Son of was around — he could stop a planet by now.

01.40.89

Awoke with a real start from fitful sleep — something was moving. My God, was something moving!! What I at first took to be a plant detached itself from the foliage and came cranking towards me — it was a massive robot. It thumped, rolled, splashed through some swamp, stopped, looked at me, then went cranking on!!

GAMMADEN 27 *02.59.89*

A city with giant spider webs and no people or traffic — then a huge comet in the sky — he's trying to scare me back *— I'm getting near him and he knows it. There were giant spider webs back awhile — well, I'll really worry when I meet the spider! Meantime I'm heading on!*

GAMMADEN 27 17.45.89

More harassment in the forest. These bulbous fruits are everywhere. Thirsty so tried a sip from one of the gourds. Tasted delicious so had a real bellyful — then the harassment began again. Some sort of swamp beastie came up in front of me — nasty shock but SOP would have had him for breakfast.

Later a ship came through the swamps. At least, I think it was a ship. By then was hallucinating badly. Definitely the jungle juice. Heavy sweats and running a high temperature. Had to ease up for a time.

Found myself back at the club, in my hostess outfit. That did it — snapped out quick. That was definitely HIM — it was so obvious. Go home little girlie. Well Joker — it's going to be on you when I find you!! Once I made that decision my head cleared almost immediately — so I was right . . .

GAMMADEN 28 *19.45.89*

I'm getting very close — I sense it — he's throwing all sorts of carrots at me — a shot-up village — still the smell of hot ammunition — a large ship — obviously supposed to be waiting to take me away. Well, all this does is to amaze me at how determined I can be when I set my face at something.

A very, very strong scent in my nose now. Another city. This time more logical — more my type of town — its outline even seems familiar. The sort of streets I would hustle in — the smell of decaying rubbish — and a very strong sense of someone just departed. He may even be here. It's so obvious — in the tower — he's always showing me towers — and I will have to climb the tower because this tired old flivver can't make more than three metres heightwise. I'm not yet sure whether to call him. If I climb the tower he'll take the flivver. On foot I'd never survive.

GAMMADEN 29   40.90.89

We meet, WE MEET!! Not face to face — that wouldn't be possible because of course he does not physically exist — but we meet in mind. I face him fully exposed for judgement. Like a fleck of dust he picks me up and draws me into his mind. 'Well J,' he asks, 'what do you think of it so far?' And I reply, 'What do you think of ME so far?' He just smiles. If he had a face it would be lined — but not too much so, a sort of mellow skin. His eyes would definitely be hidden — some sort of heat shielding because he would see worlds no one else could comprehend. And a simple helmet to protect all that energy from seeping out and fraternizing with lesser species.

'Well J,' he says again, 'where do you go from here?' 'You know exactly where I want to go,' I reply. 'Ah yes — and when you get to Earth J,' he continues, 'will that be it — will that be the end of this odyssey?' 'Who knows?' is all I can reply. I'm just about to leave when completely as an afterthought I turn and ask, 'Thingy — you know — was it purple?' He just smiles. 'Will he come to Earth as well?' But he's gone.

GAMMADEN 30   51.96.89

I made the market rendezvous with Zoe. 'So is it a building?' she asked. 'No, more a sort of shed,' I returned. Nice to see the look on her face. Using her flivver as shuttle she took me out to a passing trader going down-galaxy. I knew I was on my way. Looking back I could see this invented world — only three pieces. Funny, I thought, most rooms have four walls. Let's get on with the big one.

GAMMADEN 40   06.14.89

The trader had the most amazing pad. His own private asteroid — full air dome, the lot. Have spent a few days there. Well, you have to check these things out and he's stinking rich. Wifey hasn't taken too kindly to the intrusion, but bearing in mind the sun hasn't been too kind to her shin or brain I'm not surprised. Nik — the man — could be a useful contact. You don't get where he is without influence. Am staying for a flash party — you know — everyone arriving by private shuttle — then finally on with the serious stuff.

Standing on the deck could look back and see the old galaxy — from here it's just like a giant puffball. How it aged me — by about a million years. One of his daughters is so like me when I was a cadet. I've done a drawing of her. Bright little thing (worth a few on the markets?!) — she really reminds me of what I was like. Was tempted to try it on but one should hardly bite the hand that feeds. Via Nik I'm getting (for services rendered) use of his brand new core shuttle — 500 light years a day! — beyond comprehension. Of course, I said I'd bring it back!!!

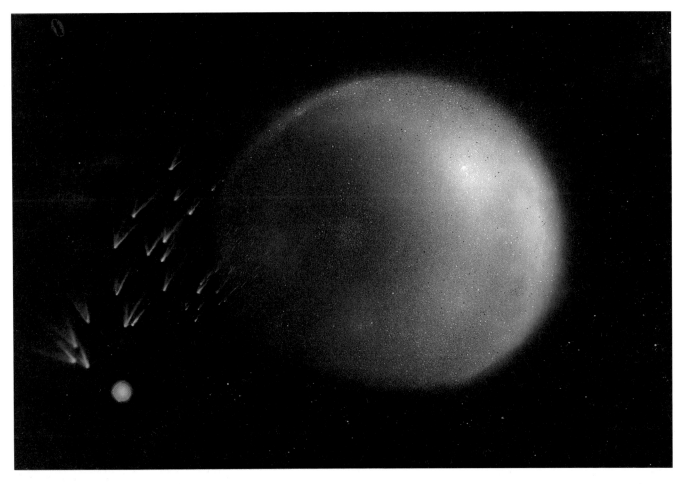

GAMMADEN 86 *18.26.89*

Even at the speed this thing moves it's been a long run. Fortunately it has all the gear so I put myself in suspension. Nik was quite the man to know. Via him, no questions asked, I got charts showing ordinance dispositions on the run in to Earth.

I'm shortly going to have to hype myself up for some astute manouvering. This thing has scanner shields and of course speed so far ahead of light only the most up-to-date screens can read it — but even so at the end of the day it's going to be my wits against whatever's out there. Wish Purple could have made it.

GAMMADEN 87   40.57.89

So far so good. Perimeter satellites almost non-existent. Had expected far more comprehensive cover. Came across a completely abandoned freighter. Most peculiar! Reactors obviously been running for eons. Lights still on but absolutely no one on board. Looks like it was abandoned in a hurry — food still on tables, charts being worked on, but dust and decomposition everywhere. Whoever left it did so a long time ago.

So far entry has been suspiciously easy. I have all sorts of ID codes to give depending on situation but so far have received absolutely no challenge.

GAMMADEN 88 *48.20.89*

Can hardly contain my excitement. Have passed with quite suspicious ease outer markers, then inner markers, and no cross beams showing on any of the scanners. I mean, back at meteorite city we had more sophisticated defence systems than this and I thought the whole universe wanted to get down to Earth — that's why they banned humans — we would have swamped the place. You only got to Earth when you were too old to appreciate it — that's why I signed that sodding contract! Anyway — think I'm needlessly paranoid.

Saw nice floating city on the way in — looks like it was coated in gold. Some of the satellites look a bit battered though — would have thought any company would have operated better than that — still, governments are always tight with money. Should feel far more pleased that things are going so well. Have one last box of tricks to program and that should get me down though I've been warned about ground sensors.

GAMMADEN 89 *52.20.89*

Can see the ground — GOD IT'S FANTASTIC — just like the old atlases. Perhaps a bit darker and browner but definitely a familiar contour sequence.

60.20.89

Am putting down near the coast. After all, I have come to see the sea haven't I? What's the first thing I'll do — SKINNYDIP! Then I'll make a very, very large sandcastle, and then I shall have tea — that's what they do on Earth I believe.

72.20.89

Touchdown! Quite effortless — looking out it could be anywhere. There's a sort of walled city with a citadel up front. I've got papers if I'm challenged.

74.20.89

Have opened the hatch. Frankly the air's a little staler than I would've expected. Almost similar to that on Stos or some other dump like that. And absolutely no grass. I wanted to jump down and roll in lush green grass — still I'm fairly near the ocean, so perhaps this is more a beach.

GAMMADEN 90 84.56.89

Have just had a VERY VERY VERY UNPLEASANT SHOCK. The beach was a real mess. AND THE WATER — I'd stripped off ready to run into the ocean when I realized the brown gunge all round the ship was the water. THE PLACE IS DEAD — deader than the foulest planet I've ever been on. There is absolutely no life here whatsoever — and the air is foul! I thought maybe with my luck I'd hit on an old industrial complex so I climbed the cliffs to get a better view of the coastline. I was just mounting a final ridge when this damn robot comes clanking up. A ROBOT! So I shot the bastard between its stupid eyes.

GAMMADEN 92 25.48.89

I am in a state of shock. I have traversed about two hundred miles of what was the Atlantic seaboard and can quite categorically report that the entire land and sea mass is totally, completely and utterly lifeless. There is the stench of decay that is impossible to shake off. The air is actually better in the ship after more than a quarter on board. Worst, and most ominous of all, the only things that move are sodding machines still fighting some crazy war — and where have I seen THAT before!!? Could this be possibly the Joker's big one — from meeting him I can't believe that. NO, THIS IS FOR REAL. Mankind has smashed this place to bits — just like it smashes everything.

GAMMADEN 93   *10.21.89*

Awoken from fitful sleep by massive explosion in remains of forest behind me. More of those bloody machines I suppose.

GAMMADEN 94   40.21.89

Just as I thought. Went through ruins of what must have been a large metropolis. One of the buildings was heavily fortified and had withstood the ravages of war and weather quite well. Inside was in quite good condition. It had been some sort of library. Records were stacked floor to ceiling in no particular order but rummaging through these and checking computer files soon confirmed the truth. As if I didn't know what it was. A fourth global war had decimated the place and the totally-changed climate evaporated massive amounts of water, lost in space through the depleted atmospheric layers. Tidal waves and earthquakes finished what man had begun and the last civilization left for other planets more than a thousand years ago. It was decided that no humans would return to Earth until the planet had revived itself, and to that end a sophisticated defence system would be installed above the planet to forstall such an event.

The rule that people in their old age could live out their last years on the planet is a fiction. Ships are sent on auto-pilot into deep space with their geriatric cargo — returning when all on board have died for lack of air to be secretly incinerated. Nothing can surprise me now.

GAMMADEN 95   05.47.89

Have thought this through really carefully. There is absolutely no point in carrying on. The whole purpose of everything was to get here — all the lying, cheating, hustling, ripping people off — the lot — was always with one end in mind — to get here. To prove I could do it, but above all to sit by a clear blue sea with a clear blue sky above. To breathe the silky-smooth mother air, not the fabricated muck we have in space. It does not exist — so what's the point. I've got some nice little pills on the ship. I'm told they taste nice and they're very quick. So tomorrow I shall have a last smoke, a last walkabout and then pop off.

GAMMADEN 96

Totally totally smashed on all my stash of strike in one big ball. I can hear the Joker — I can even see him — is he laughing or crying? His face comes and goes. Other more confusing images — a minotaur of all things with beautiful coloured wings. It's crying as well. I think it's saying: This is who I could have been given the chance. I would have swooped in the sunlight — I would have dazzled you with my grace and speed but instead man built machines to try and do the same thing. How can man possibly duplicate nature. Now he has no home he will smash his way across space.

Perhaps the Joker was an Earthman. And that's why he created that great building — it's the museum of Earth. Everything that was beautiful and idyllic he tried to preserve but other Earth people got in and nibbled at the edges. The flying people are the minotaurs breed, nibbling at the fat merchants exploiting the shed's resources.

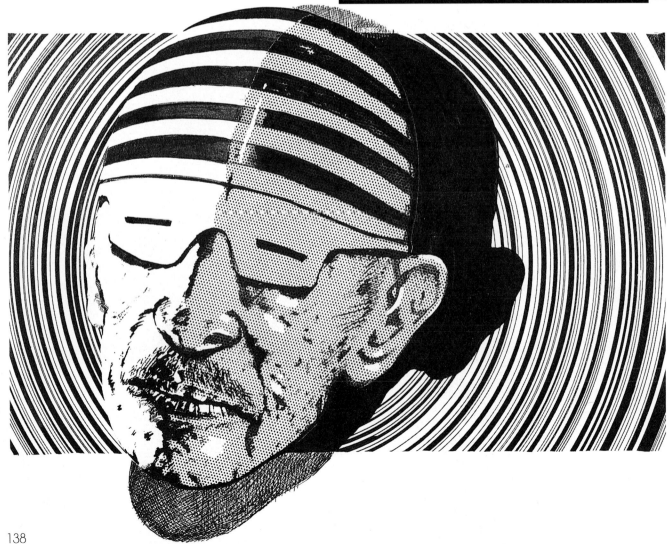

GAMMADEN 97 *14.20.89*

Funny quirky things come into my mind. How quaint and innocent those first space settlers looked in the library records. A bit like me. They were going out into that amazing new frontier land full of hope and expectation for the future, both for themselves and those that would follow — if they could have known what their explorations and machinations would lead to would they have started it all? Why didn't we just stay up in the trees, smoke spliffs and chat to each other?

37.46.89

Can't bear to watch another sunset. That seedy yellow orb that just plops into the brown muck on the horizon! How I hate the colour brown. The colour of wind, strike, army equipment . . . If I was going to have a home of my own it would be all blue — everything — every surface — blue blue blue.

This stuff is so good. That's what really makes the world go round — except they even go to war over that — what a stupid race — what a really stupid race . . .

GAMMADEN 98 49.50.89

My final hours. Two last self-portraits beside the first one I ever did. How young, silly, but totally self-confident and hopeful I look in that drawing! How could I have imagined what was to come?

20.19.89

SOMETHING HAS HAPPENED! I went down to the shore before taking the pills driven by some strange sixth sense. There in the mud were these gigantic prints. It could only be SON OF PURPLE! Perhaps that huge explosion the other night was him making entry!

I breasted a rise and there he was, and guess what — all around him in what passes for the dawn light here I could see little green shoots glimmering! Wherever his scales are falling — and he's moulting a lot — they're taking root and beginning to sprout! There was an absolute sea of them behind his tail. At this rate the whole valley will be seeded within the month. Then maybe trees will follow — and possibly rain . . . Joker?

ALPHADEN 12 02.45.90

Almost a year has passed since that last entry. Looking from the window I can see a green prairie. The air has improved and once in a while we get rainfall. This is my last drawing, a self-portrait — have I seen this face before?